Mighty Stallion 3

Glory's Legend

Follow in the hoof prints of Sariavo's grandson, Glory…

………Glory had so much to live up to being the son of Fury and the grandson of the great Sariavo. His life would lead him on the road of great friendship and he would find that true love could be stronger than anything else…..

Mighty Stallion 3

Glory's Legend

The Sequel to Mighty Stallion 2 Fury's Journey

By: Victoria Kasten

Original cover by James Krom Natural Images

Mighty Stallion 3
Glory's Legend

Second Printing • 500 copies • October 2008

Library of Congress
Control Number: 2005909573

ISBN: 978-0-9788850-2-1

Additional copies of this book are available. See back pages for information. Send comments/payments to:
5465 Glencoe Ave
Webster, MN 55088

Published By: Victoria Kasten
www.EpicScrolls.com

Printed in the USA by
Morris Publishing
3212 East Highway 30
Kearney, NE 68847
1-800-650-7888

To: Grandpa Richard and Grandma Sharon Krom
And Grandma Ilene Kasten

Thank you all for your unending supply of support and love!

TABLE OF CONTENTS

~ 1 ~

Footsteps to Follow

Glory sighed. Would he ever get the urge to leave his parents and have his own adventures? His thoughts strayed to a faraway place, with a beautiful mare, that he had to find.

"Glory, your grandsire wants you to come inside!" his mother Novana called to him from the entrance to the cave that was their home.

Glory reluctantly stood up, shook himself, and started towards the cave that was the size of a small town. He entered, and saw his father and grandfather, Fury and Sariavo, swimming happily in the indoor pool.

Sariavo looked up and saw his grandson. "Glory! Come and join us." Glory grinned at them and slipped into the water. Immediately he felt himself being pushed down under the water. He fought frantically, and suddenly the weight on his shoulders disappeared. He rose above the water, and saw his father laughing.

"You pushed me down, didn't you, Dad?" he asked. Fury nodded.

"Are you going to do something about it?" his father teased.

Glory grinned. "Yup." He promptly swam over to his sire, and dunked the older stallion. When Fury came up again, he sputtered angrily.

"Why, you…"

Glory laughed. "Are you going to do something about it?" he said, mimicking his father's words.

Fury laughed. Novana pretended to be horrified. "Oh, no! My son has his father's sense of humor."

This brought chuckles from around the large entrance room.

Glory stepped out of the pool. He motioned the two other stallions out of the way, and then backed up for a running start. He ran straight at the pool, and jumped high in the air. His body crashed into the water, spraying water over everyone. When he came up, he heard laughter from the horses behind him. He grinned.

"Thank you, thank you very much!"

Fury snorted. "I could do that. It's not that hard." Glory could tell that his father was teasing, but still, there seemed to be a tiny part of the comment that was serious.

He squared his shoulders, which is very hard to do in the water, and said, "Okay, Dad. I challenge you to do better."

Fury nodded. "I will." With that, he climbed out of the water and backed to the far wall. Then he raced at the pool. When he neared the edge, he hesitated, and fell forward into a belly flop. The cracking sound of his body hitting the water chilled Glory down to his bones. Was his father all right?

Then, a bright red face appeared above the water. Fury gasped. "Ouch."

Glory chuckled softly. "Dad, that was..." Fury made a face at his son.

"I know. It wasn't very graceful."

Glory shook his head. "You are tougher than I thought, Dad." Fury's laugh echoed through the cave walls.

****

Glory felt restless. He didn't know why, and he wasn't sure what to do. All of his favorite places in and around the cave were suddenly dull and boring.

Was this the feeling his father said he would get when it was time for him to have his adventure? He decided to ask his grandfather, Sariavo. He walked into the cave, past the pool, past his room, his parents' room, from which came soft snores, and finally his grandmothers' rooms.

The very last chamber on the long hallway was the largest. Here was the room that Sariavo called his own.

Glory felt uncomfortable. He had never entered this room, and his grandsire had never asked him in, so would he be angry with his grandson for going in? Glory shuddered, and tapped the entrance with his forefoot.

"Grandfather? Can I come in?" Glory called into the darkness.

"Glory? Is that you? Come on in! I'm always glad to talk to my grandson."

Glory sighed. He was glad that his grandfather wasn't angry with him for invading his privacy. He stepped into the room, and a small hole in the ceiling lit the area just enough so he could see.

Glory saw a small pool in one corner, and a big flat rock in the other. The rock was used as a table. His grandsire was lying in the pool, which was barely two feet deep. The pool was used to sooth aches and bruises away, as well as simply a place to relax.

The old stallion smiled. "What's on your mind, Glory?" he asked softly.

"I'm restless, Grandfather. Its like I have to go somewhere but I'm…" Glory hung his head.

"You don't know why, when, or where?" Sariavo said. Glory's head shot up.

"Yeah, but how do you know?" he questioned. Sariavo chuckled.

"Remember, I was your age once. I had the same feeling. It's time for you to go on a journey. And it would also help," Sariavo paused, "to find a heart to match yours."

Glory gulped. "A…mare?"

Sariavo nodded. "Yes, that has been my greatest pleasure. Sari and Penny add so much joy to my life," he said, and then laughed merrily.

Glory shook himself. "Thank you for letting me speak with you, Grandfather. I think I'll take a walk in the morning to think it over."

~ 2 ~

Glory Meets Man

Glory woke himself early in the morning. He trotted briskly out of the cave. He was looking forward to being a lone for a while to think things over.

Suddenly, a small chestnut filly came flying out of the cave. "Take me with you, please Glory?" his younger sister, Inahu, asked frantically.

Glory started in surprise at her sudden appearance, and then smiled at her. "You'll have to ask Mother and Dad. If they agree, I'll take you."

The filly turned and almost ran into her mother. "Mom, can I please go with Glory, I'm almost two years old?"

Novana laughed. "Are you that eager to go? There are dangers, you know."

Inahu nodded. "I know, but I'm strong, and Glory can take care of me."

Novana looked at her son. "Glory, are you sure you want to take her? She might be a handful."

Glory nodded again. "Sure, why not? I'll keep her in line."

Novana shook her head. "Youngsters. Go ahead, Inahu. Be good."

Inahu yelped, and jumped up in the air. "You're not excited are you?" Glory asked teasingly.

As soon as Glory and Inahu were out of sight of the herd, Inahu started up a steady chatter, and told Glory everything she thought they would see. "…a bear's den, maybe a human, a human house, a real cougar, a big wolf…" Glory soon wished he could plug his ears. "Enough!" he growled.

Inahu stared at him. "What's wrong, Glory?" she asked.

"You! You can't keep chattering, or you'll wear my ears down to stubs. Be quiet for a while, please."

Inahu's lower lip began to tremble. "I'm, sorry." She said, her voice shaky. Glory rolled his eyes, but then he felt something, as though they were being watched.

He didn't dare turn his head. "Inahu," he whispered, "Don't move." Inahu froze instantly.

Glory slowly turned his head. What he saw made him jump; a human sat on a big buckskin gelding, and was watching him. Glory laced his ears back, and moved between the man and his little sister.

The brave grinned. "That is a sight I wouldn't expect to see. A stallion caring for a foal?"

Inahu gasped. "But I'm not a foal, I'm-" Glory cut her off. "Be quiet, Inahu."

The Indian moved his hand down towards his belt. Glory saw a rope coiled there.

"Inahu, when I say run, you go back to the herd as fast as you can. Tell Dad that I need help." His sister nodded. The hand came up, with it, the rope. "Now!" Glory yelled at the chestnut filly. Inahu took off like a streak of lightning.

Glory backed slowly away, until the horse and rider started to follow him. Glory knew that he couldn't lead this human back to the herd, because if he did, all the horses would be in danger.

He faked a rush, and then sped away from the herd. To his anger and surprise, the brave went after Inahu! Glory whirled and took after the other horse. As soon as he was abreast of the other horse, he reared and knocked the rider clear off his horse. The man yelled with fear and surprise, and rolled clear of the pounding hooves. He jumped back to his horse, and swung his rope. Glory felt it brush against his ears, and jumped sideways. He sped away, towards a clearing.

He stopped to see if the Indian had followed him, and was satisfied to hear hoof beats behind him. He leaned against a tree trunk, and suddenly, an arrow sped over his head and buried itself in a tree behind him.

Glory jumped and whirled, and saw the Indian sitting under a pine tree, holding a bow and arrow. Glory didn't think that the brave would kill him, because he was a rare find. White stallions were the kind of horse that the Indians idolized.

Glory was suddenly aware of another presence. Fury, his father, came bellowing out of the trees. Inahu was hiding behind a big rock, so the Indian wouldn't see her.

Fury sped right towards the deadly bow and arrows. Glory yelled, "Dad! Stop!" but his warning came too late. Fury whirled sideways, but an arrow struck his shoulder. The red stallion stopped, shuddered, and fell to his knees.

Glory was filled with such a rage that he drove at the Indian sideways. Inahu, seeing the danger her brother was in, distracted the brave by stepping away from the rock. Glory hit the Indian from the side, and was rewarded by getting an arrow stuck into his chest. Glory gasped for breath, then slowly fell to his knees. Inahu screamed, and raced to her brother.

She dropped beside him, and licked away some of the blood. She frantically spoke to him, "Glory? Did he kill you? Glory please don't die!"

He gasped again, and looked up at her. "I'm not dead yet, Inahu."

Fury was standing by this time and charging the Indian again. The brave took one look at the infuriated horse, and leaped to his horse's back, galloping away.

Inahu was sobbing over Glory, her tears splattering in a small pool on the grass. Fury marched right over to them. "Glory? Are you okay?"

Glory gasped softly, and nodded. Fury grasped the long feathered end of the arrow in his teeth.

Around clenched teeth, he said, "Glory, don't move. Inahu, get a leaf or something to stop the blood flow out of his chest." Inahu grabbed a large fern, and poised it over the arrow. Glory bit his lip sharply, and closed his eyes. Fury gripped the arrow tightly, and then shot straight back, so the arrow wouldn't hook onto Glory's muscles. Glory made a grimace, and exhaled slowly. Inahu had pressed the fern against her brother's chest, and red blood had seeped through the frail leaf.

After a few minutes, Fury helped the younger stallion up, and supported his son on his shoulder. Glory arched his neck over his sire's back, and saw the arrow sticking out of the red shoulder. "Dad! We have to pull your arrow out too," Glory said.

Fury shook his head. "No, your mother will help me with that. You are injured worse than I am. We are getting you home."

Inahu trotted next to Glory. "Are you sure you're all right?"

The white colt grinned. "I'm made of steel, remember?" She laughed, a bright, twinkling sound that filled Glory's ears like music.

When they reached the cave, Novana took one look at the two wounded stallions, and marched right over. "Fury! Glory! What on earth did you two mix with this time?" Fury grinned, and grunted softly as his mare pulled the arrow out of his shoulder.

"May I help you?" a soft rippling voice said. Glory's eyes widened as he saw a buckskin filly making her way through the crowd that had gathered around Fury and his son. She smiled at Glory, and he felt his heart flop to his hooves. “My name is Secret. I just came here to visit my uncle. The gelding Jake is my mother’s brother.”

She looked at his chest, and gasped. She looked at Fury. “Fury? I will see that he is taken care of, if you don’t mind.” Fury gave Glory a wink and a look that said, ‘she’s got you roped and tied’, and nodded.

Secret slowly eased her body under Glory’s shoulder, and helped him into the cave. He groaned softly as she let him slowly fall into a bed of moss on the floor of his room.

She nudged a turtle shell full of water next to him, and started gently cleaning the bloody hole. Glory gasped as the water stung his chest, then was immediately embarrassed at showing his hurt in front of a girl.

If Secret had noticed, she didn’t show it. Her hoof barely touched the hurt area, dripping water over it. She lifted her dark eyes to his, and Glory felt his instincts flare. Was this what Sariavo had told him about? “A heart to match your own.”

Glory didn’t realize he had spoken aloud until he heard Secret say, “Is that what you want, Glory?” He stared at her.

“Yes. I don’t even know you, but already I…I like you.” She laughed.

“Well, thank you. I like you too. I’m here for three months, and then I leave. Will you show me your territory?" Glory nodded, breathless at the beauty of this filly's eyes.

Secret lifted her muzzle and blew softly into Glory's face. "You know me. I have never been far from you. Did you see me when you were fighting the Indian? And when you spoke to Inahu on the trail? I watched you in secret from the trees." Glory frowned. "I didn't see you."

Secret's eyelashes lifted slightly. "We were born to be together, Glory. God created us to be each other's. I loved you from the day I was old enough to know that someone special was waiting for me. I didn't know who, but I knew eventually I would meet him. I believe that stallion is you, Glory."

~ 3 ~

Broken Dreams

The day after his fight, Glory was well enough to stand and walk around. Secret had woken every few hours to check his injury.

When he began to feel better, he insisted on showing her around the cave, and so he did. He showed her all the rooms, the pools, the game fields, and the huge swimming pool.

****

Glory slipped into the clear water, letting it sooth his aches. He was barely aware of Secret sliding in next to him. Inahu was swimming at the other end, and paddled over when she saw them. She stopped a few feet away and looked from Glory to Secret, then back to Glory. She giggled, and started to chant: "Glory and Secret sitting in the pool, K-I-S-S-I-"

She never finished. Her seventeen hand high brother dunked her under the water, and rocketed her to the other end again. She scrambled out of the pool, laughing, and ran to her mother. Novana rolled her eyes, and shrugged. Sariavo watched the proceedings with a twinkle in his eyes.

****

Secret was an excellent nurse, and by the end of the week, Glory was well enough to show her more of his world. They took walks in the woods, swam under the waterfall at the entrance of the cave, and galloped across the endless expanse of prairie. Secret grew dearer to Glory every day, and she became part of his life. Glory was so entranced by the buckskin filly, that he spent less and less time with his family.

Inahu confronted Glory one day, and said boldly, "You are so awful! You used to spend time with me every day, and now everything is Secret, Secret, Secret, and I am sick of the way you are ignoring everyone!"

Glory was startled at her outcry, and countered, "Inahu, you aren't old enough to understand what love does to you, and once you find your stallion, you will see why everything is Secret, Secret, Secret!"

Inahu's lower lip began to tremble, and she glared up at Glory defiantly. "Fine, you just stay with your precious Secret, and see if I care!" With that, the yearling filly marched off. Glory slowly walked back to the woods, where Secret was waiting for him.

****

Glory went to find Secret, with thoughts whirling around his mind. He saw her swimming with Inahu, the two of them playing water tag, laughing like young foals. Glory stopped at the edge of the pool, and spoke to Secret, "Secret? Can I talk to you, please?" Secret gracefully stepped out of the pool, and walked over to Glory.

He was about to speak, when Sariavo trumpeted, "We have visitors!!!" Glory and Secret ran to the mouth of the cave, and saw three exhausted horses galloping towards them.

One of the horses, an old stallion, was leading a black mare, and a blood bay filly. Glory had never seen such a beautiful color of bay in his life. He stepped forward, ducking under the filly just as she collapsed onto his back.

He overheard the old stallion speaking to Sariavo.

"Thank you so much for letting us intrude on your home, sir. We were chased by a group of humans and barely managed to escape from our own territory without being caught."

Glory shook his head in disgust of the humans, lifted the filly as if she weighed no more than a feather, and carried her to a spare room. She sank to the moss bed, and sighed.

Glory was transfixed. Secret was beautiful, but this filly was PERFECTION. Her beautifully crafted head was slightly dished, showing an Arabian heritage. Her slender legs sported four white socks, and a stripe of white ran down her face.

****

When her eyelids fluttered open, Glory felt as if she could read his mind. She gasped, "Where am I…who are you?"

Glory gulped, trying to regain his voice. "I…I am G…Glory. You came to my cave…my grandfather's cave." Glory felt like kicking himself. What a lame answer.

She gazed at him wordlessly. "You are a rare sight, Mighty Stallion." Glory stared at her. Sariavo had been called the same thing.

He turned to see Secret standing in the doorway. "Hello, what is your name?" she asked the other filly.

"Gabrielle. I am the daughter of the stallion Wildfire." Glory smiled at Secret. "Time for our walk? We should let Gabrielle get some rest."

****

Two days later, Glory asked Gabrielle to walk to the waterfall with him, and she obliged. Secret had been fairly silent the last two days, but hadn't objected to Glory when he had canceled their swimming date.

Now, he was basking in the sunlight with the most beautiful filly he had ever seen. Gabrielle was amazing. She was smart, gorgeous, and funny. She loved to act, and Glory encouraged her to try new accents and impersonations. She did his father once, walking in a funny duck looking pace. Glory laughed so hard he cried.

Gabrielle was now the center of Glory's life. He spent every waking moment with her. He didn't seem to notice Secret anymore. She watched the couple from a distance, but never intruded. Novana felt sorry for her, and tried to make her feel included in social activities.

Secret covered her misery well, but she still could be heard softly crying at night. Glory was so busy with Gabrielle, that he never noticed Secret when she came to bring him food or messages. He always was talking to the bay filly.

****

Finally, one day, Glory decided that Gabrielle was the mare that would make him most happy, and walked into the woods to their secret place to ask her to marry him. He stopped when he heard soft voices carrying to him over the hedge of sumac that hid the small nook that was so special to him.

He peeked around the corner to see Gabrielle muzzle to muzzle with one of the young stallions in his father's herd, Patch. Patch was a tall, leggy, black and white paint, and very handsome.

Glory whirled, and ran away from the cave, Gabrielle, and his broken dreams. He flew along the prairie where Gabrielle had told him she loved him more than anything. He ran past the big hill where Fury had appeared with his herd three years ago. He ran for four miles, until he collapsed on the ground, bellowing his rage and hurt.

He knew he had to get away from everything that reminded him of Gabrielle. He needed to go far, far away. He stood, looked back the way he had come, for what he thought to be the last time, and cantered on, breathing heavily.

Glory traveled for three days without stopping except to eat and nap for an hour or two. He was so oblivious to everything except his grief and pain.

It was about three-o-clock in the afternoon when he came upon a herd of six mares grazing peacefully in a sheltered valley. He lifted his head, and whistled a greeting. The mares looked up, and whinnied excitedly. He trotted down the trail to them, and they hurried over to meet him.

The lead mare, a pretty palomino, bowed respectfully. Glory was suspicious. "Don't you have a stallion?" he asked, warily. The mare shook her head. "No, he was killed by a grizzly bear up in the mountain. We are alone. Will you be our stallion?"

Glory grinned. "I just happen to need a herd, so yes. What is your name?" The mare smiled. "My name is Grace, and I am nineteen years old. The herd has been in my care until now. I gladly surrender my position."

Glory moved his new family up into the mountains, and down the other side, into another valley.

Now, unknown to Glory, a large Indian settlement lay just on the other side of the canyon wall.

~ 4 ~

At The End of a Rope

Just as the sun peeked over the canyon, a group of bronze skinned riders appeared in the bottom of the canyon, riding spotted horses. They whispered excitedly as they saw the six good-looking mares and the prized albino stallion. They pulled their ropes out of leather saddlebags, taken from the ruins of a stagecoach, and moved silently forward.

Glory couldn't smell them, because the wind was moving away from him toward the Indians. He slept heavily, unaware of the coming danger.

When the Indians struck, not one of the horses was awake. At the first sound of the whooping humans, they all jumped up and fled toward the trail leading out of the canyon.

A young gray mare stumbled and fell, and was quickly picked off by one of the braves. The other six horses sped on, trying their utmost to stay ahead of their pursuers.

Glory saw a rope settle around Grace's neck, pulling her to a stop. Finally, all the mares were gone, leaving Glory to flee alone.

A muscular, warrior looking Indian galloped after Glory, his rope coiled and ready. Glory whirled sharply to run into a small, box canyon. In an instant, he saw his mistake. Three walls surrounded him. The trail was a dead end.

He turned to see the Indian ride slowly into the canyon, his rope held high. Glory screamed angrily, not wanting to be a prisoner.

The rope flew over Glory's neck. The young stallion bucked and reared, fighting the warrior. The Indian held on to the rope, letting the albino wear himself out. Once Glory saw there was no escape, he stopped fighting the rope, and let his hate show as he glared at the human who held him captive.

The man began to lead Glory back to the settlement. Glory did not struggle, knowing it to be useless. But as they went, Glory vowed to get his mares and himself free as soon as possible.

****

When the group of Indians with their newly captured herd of horses reached the village, the chief walked out to see the stallion the other warriors had told him about. His face curved up in a smile as he saw the prize brought forward. "This will be my spirit horse, and I will never be wounded, because he will protect me."

(The Indians thought that riding such horses turned away instruments meant to kill them.)

The chief stepped a foot away from Glory, and named him, "White Horse." The chief turned, and walked back to his tepee.

****

During the days that followed, Glory learned from conversation among his captors that his 'master' was a younger chief, and that his name was Running Fox. The Indian came to see him daily, giving him apples from a tree in the middle of the village. Glory never let the man touch him, but watched every step Running Fox made.

By the end of the week, Glory had decided the chief was not going to hurt him, and Running Fox was able to touch his prize, whispering soothing words to the stallion. "White Horse, you and I will be made into legends for our bravery in battle. Your beauty and courage will be remembered in the hearts of my people. I will never let you fall."

Glory sighed. His life wasn't so bad. The people in the village idolized him, and the children came to bring him sweet things to eat. Running Fox was kind to him, and acted as though Glory were a human.

Running Fox had painted a sun on Glory's left shoulder, and dipped his hand in blue paint and placed his handprint on Glory's right hip, and he tied an eagle feather in Glory's mane to show that he was the horse of a chief.

****

Running Fox looped a rope bridle through Glory's mouth. The albino tossed his head in confusion. "Easy, White Horse. I won't hurt you."

Glory grabbed the bridle in his teeth, and threw it to the ground. A look of understanding passed through Running Fox's eyes. "I will ride you without any aids. You will be as free as an eagle. But promise me that you will be loyal to me."

Glory nodded his head solemnly. Running Fox gently settled onto Glory's back. The young horse stood calmly. "Good boy, White Horse."

But their newfound friendship was soon interrupted by something.

****

Early one morning, a scout raced past Glory's tie rope. "Comanche warriors coming over the ridge! Get your horses ready!"

As if out of thin air, Running Fox suddenly appeared beside Glory. The Indian untied the stallion's tie rope, and jumped on Glory's back. A squaw handed him a tomahawk, then she ran to join the parade of women and children fleeing the village. Running Fox dug his feet into the stallion's flank, yelling, "Go, White Horse!"

The two joined the line of warriors, and the chief called for the warriors to charge. Glory raced forward with his fellows, intent on destroying the raiders. A yelling, paint smeared Comanche headed for Running Fox, waving his tomahawk. Running Fox whooped and brought his tomahawk down on the enemy, and then the pair raced on, Running Fox brandishing his weapon.

At the end of the battle, Running Fox and his men were the victors. All but three of the thirty-eight Comanche warriors were dead or dying. Glory heaved long breaths, his nostrils filled with the scents of battle.

He barely noticed that a long gash from a tomahawk decorated his shoulder. Running Fox, however, saw it right away, and leaped from his stallion's back. He cleaned off the cut with a deerskin rag, and slowly led his horse back to the tie rope.

Once there, he petted and talked to the horse, feeding him grapes and apples. "White Horse, you are the source of all bravery. You are courageous in battle. That is the greatest trait found in a horse."

After that, Running Fox never tied Glory to the stake, but left him to graze freely. In gratitude for this great honor, Glory never strayed far from his master.

****

One afternoon, Grace paid him a visit. She had become the mount of one of the squaws, and was content to remain so. "Hello White Horse. You are quite famous, now. I've heard stories from the Indians of you racing alone into battle, fire spurting from your nose and eyes."

Glory laughed. "That is ridiculous."

Grace smiled. "Maybe. It has come to my attention that you have not even attempted to escape. I must say that surprises me."

Glory shook his head. "No, Running Fox is good to me, and, I'm happy here." Grace nodded. She said goodbye, and left.

Glory thought about what Grace had told him. Fire spurting from his eyes? How silly can people be? He honestly hadn't thought much about leaving, and he had been truthful when he'd said that he was happy.

As Glory's thoughts continued though, the image of a buckskin filly entered his mind. She looked at him with pain in her eyes, and a tear escaped her eyelid.

Another horse appeared beside her, and Glory recognized his father. Fury had hurt showing on his face, and he made soft noises to Secret, trying to comfort her.

In the background, his grandfather looked at Glory, his voice carrying over the depths of Glory's mind. "Why did you leave us, Glory? Come home, my grandson!" The vision was suddenly gone, leaving Glory with a puzzled expression.

~ 5 ~

Let Freedom Ring

A pink cloud covered the sun, moving behind the canyon walls. The sunset reminded Glory of the sunsets seen from the woods behind his cave. He sighed, lying in the grass beside Running Fox's tepee. If only the reminders of home would stop driving his mind crazy. He was starting to miss his parents…and Secret.

His restlessness was not unnoticed by his master, and the Indian chief was starting to worry about his prized stallion.

Running Fox went out to see Glory. He brought a wild strawberry to give to the albino stallion. Glory accepted the treat with gratitude, and then resumed staring into the sunset.

Running Fox frowned with worry. This wasn't like White Horse at all. The stallion was usually lively and proud. Now, he gazed into the clouds with a sense of sadness and pain.

Glory bent his neck around to nuzzle Running Fox's chest. The Indian ran a gentle hand down the white muzzle.

Running Fox leaped to Glory's back, and rode him farther down the valley.

When they got to the trail leading up out of the canyon, Running Fox dismounted, and patted Glory's neck. "White Horse, you are a wild stallion, not meant to be prisoner of men. I give back to you the freedom I stole. You are free to go. Do not forget me, White Horse."

Glory didn't believe his ears. He felt torn between his two worlds. He wanted to go back, but he also felt a desire to stay with Running Fox.

Then, he heard Secret's voice in his head. "Glory! Please, come back to me. You left me once, for Gabrielle, do not leave me alone forever."

Glory made up his mind. He reached around to his tail, and pulled out several pure white hairs, and dropped them into Running Fox's hands. The Indian smiled, and quickly braided the hair into a bracelet, and knotted it around his wrist. "I will wear this forever, White Horse, and it will be buried with me."

Running Fox took the eagle feather from his headband, and securely knotted it in Glory's mane beside the first. "Never take it off. Remember me." With that, the young brave turned and started the long walk back to camp.

Glory gave a last whinny, and raced to his master's side, and Running Fox leaped up on his back for one last ride. Glory gave every ounce of speed he had, and they flew along the ground, until they reached the village.

Glory waited until his friend dismounted and walked into his tepee. Then, he whirled and raced back to the trail.

When Glory was on his way, he thought about the last month of his life. He would forever remember the lessons in loyalty he had learned. He felt horrible about leaving Secret for Gabrielle, and foolish for not seeing that she was not true and faithful to him.

Secret was probably already married to a far more deserving stallion than himself. If she was, he still had to apologize. He also needed to apologize to his parents and grandparents for leaving them so suddenly, and without any warning. They probably thought him dead. He galloped forward, wishing he had never left.

He stopped abruptly, because he saw a group of men coming towards him. They were different than the Indians, because they wore strange hats, and while the red men rode bareback, these men rode above hunks of leather strapped on their mounts. The horses looked tough and mean.

A rope swished over his head, and Glory's short-lived freedom, was gone. The men laughed, and one of them strapped a saddle on his back so fast, Glory didn't know what was on top of him before the man was on his back.

Glory was confused and angry, because Running Fox treated him with respect, but these men treated him with disrespect and acted like he was something that could be made sport of. He bucked so wildly that the man was thrown.

The cowboy stood, dusted off his chaps, and gazed with awe at the albino stallion. "Ain't ne'er been a hoss as could throw Billy Robbins!" The other cowboys were just as surprised. "Hey! We could make some good money bettin' that some o' the boys in town couldn't stay on this here demon!" The others agreed.

****

Glory found himself trapped in a small corral, wearing a saddle, cinch, and bridle, with dozens of curious eyes staring at him over the fence. Three cowboys were lined up at the gate, waiting to ride the 'Demon'.

They smiled, made bets, and stared. The first cowboy didn't fare much better than Billy Robbins, and neither did the second. Glory's captors made a bet that the person that could ride him could take him home.

A huge, muscular man mounted Glory, and no matter how hard the stallion bucked and lunged, the man stayed on. The crowd that had gathered cheered loudly, and grudgingly, Glory's captors gave up the ownership of their money making scheme.

Glory's new owner was a mustang breeder, and he was excited to get Glory because he knew that such a stallion would greatly benefit his outfit. Glory was soon in a comfortable stall, with a blue halter around his head. He saw that he had his own private paddock. He raced outside, and saw pastures and pastures full of mares, foals, weanlings, yearlings, and other stallions.

The other stallions challenged him loudly, screaming defiance at this rogue newcomer. The foals expressed only a little interest, and the mares none at all.

Glory was depressed. Just when he had gained back his priceless freedom, he lost it.

He was surprised to see a small man coming to the paddock gate with a blue rope in his hand. Glory warily drew back, reacting to the new smell, and the rope. The man spoke softly to the stallion, never raising his eyes, and so seeming threatening.

He slowly clipped the lead line to the stallion's halter, and led him to a covered barn, where two men waited with a saddle and bridle. His new owner showed up, smiling and rubbing his hands together. "I just want to see how he acts around a saddle, and if all goes well I might have a new cow horse…"

Glory was led towards the saddle. He smelled it, and shook his head. He didn't like the smell. He tried to back away. But the man holding his lead rope didn't let him back up. That made Glory even more frustrated. He reared, knocking over the small man, and dashing past his owner. The lead rope dangled dangerously down by his hooves, and one of his forefeet came down on the long rope. The halter snapped, and Glory was free! He bolted down the gravel path, towards the road.

He kept going for days, and the miles seemed to disappear beneath his pounding hooves, towards the valley where he had found his mare herd.

Glory continued traveling until; finally, he reached the cave entrance. He looked at the red stallion dozing beside the waterfall. It was Fury, his father. Glory gently tapped Fury's shoulder with his hoof.

Fury jerked awake, and his eyes widened when he saw who it was. "Glory! My son." The older stallion gazed at his son, his expression saddening when he saw the scar from the tomahawk, and becoming curious when he saw the feather knotted in Glory's white mane.

"You have met man. An Indian has left a scar on you for the rest of your life. This makes me sad, Glory. Tell me everything." Glory began, telling his father all of his adventures.

Once again he saw Gabrielle in the thicket with Patch, found his herd, was trapped in the canyon, captured, and made the friend of Running Fox.

His father's eyes widened when Glory reached the battle, and smiled when he heard the bravery of his son. Glory told of being freed from his master, of the sadness he felt in leaving Running Fox, and being captured again.

Fury shook his head. "You are barely three years old, and yet you have already had three masters."

Glory sighed. "Where is Secret?" His father didn't get a chance to tell him, for at that moment, a blood bay filly threw herself at Glory.

It was Gabrielle. "Oh, Glory! You're back! You're safe. Why did you leave me?" She rattled the string of words so fast, that Glory had to decipher what she had said.

"I left you because you are no longer mine. I saw you that day, in the thicket, with Patch, and that is why I left."

Gabrielle's expression changed to defense. "Well…I… what does that matter? It didn't mean anything! I only stayed with him because you were gone. I am still yours, Glory."

Glory shook his head, and moved away from her towards the buckskin filly standing a few yards away. "Secret," he whispered. She looked up at him, tears rolling down her cheeks, and her shoulders shook with emotion.

"Secret, I…" Glory said no more, but rested his forehead against hers. "I was wrong to leave you, and if you will accept my apology, you can be free of me."

Secret shuddered. "I don't want to be free of you. I am your matching spirit. To leave you would be death for me. I want to be beside you for the rest of my life."

Glory looked into her eyes, and she looked back, until Glory couldn't stand it any longer. Once again the beauty of her eyes captured him. His nose inched closer to hers with every breath, and she closed her eyes. Just as they were about to touch muzzles, Gabrielle shoved Secret back, away from Glory.

"No! He is mine! You can't take him, because he loves ME!" Secret glared at the other filly, and tried to get back to Glory.

Gabrielle reared and smashed her hooves down on Secret's back. Secret screamed, and fell to her knees.

Glory flattened his ears and charged Gabrielle. The blood bay filly fell to the ground at the fierceness of his charge, and begged, "I didn't mean it, she…I…" Glory grabbed her by the mane and shoved her away from Secret.

"Get your little self-centered being away from here! Take your family with you." Glory then headed for Patch, and made him follow. "You go with her, you traitor!"

Glory stood, watching them leave, and heaving deep breaths. He looked at Secret, who was gasping for air.

~ 6 ~

Glory's Secret

Glory raced to her side, praying that she would be okay. "Secret? Please, forgive me, I should have been more watchful. I knew she would object to us," Glory pleaded. Secret lifted her eyes to his and shook her head.

"It wasn't…your fault…Glory." She slowly stood, shook herself, and grimaced. Glory saw a bruise already swelling on her back. The whole herd was out of the cave by now, and murmuring among themselves.

Novana stepped forward. "Give her to me, and I'll make sure she gets good care." Glory shook his head to stop her. "She cared for me when I was hurt. Now I must return the favor." He gently helped Secret into his own room. She lay down in the shallow pool, and she sighed appreciatively as the warm water soothed her back.

Glory stood guard over the buckskin filly all night. Whenever she groaned in pain, he talked to her of his adventures.

She could imagine the scene when he described the Comanche warrior that had attacked Running Fox, all besmeared with yellow, red and blue greasy paint. She cried when he told her that as soon as Running Fox had freed him, the cowboys had roped him and used him for sport.

****

On the third day after Gabrielle had left, Glory allowed Secret to get up and swim in the big pool, and walk a little in the woods. When he went to the woods to pick her a wildflower, he stopped at the thicket.

He hadn't been there since he'd seen Gabrielle with Patch. He started when he saw, lying in the dirt, a pure red rose. It was the most gorgeous flower he had ever seen.

He sniffed the air, and whistled angrily when he recognized the scent. Gabrielle. He pawed the dirt, and jumped when he heard soft footsteps behind him. He whirled and saw a dark shape standing just outside the thicket.

The blood bay filly stepped into the sunlight, the warm rays radiating off her beautiful body. "Hello, Glory. I thought maybe you would change your mind when you saw how loyal I am. I never left you."

Glory rolled his eyes. "What do you want, Gabrielle. I told you that we are finished. I do not love you." She smiled. "But we are not perfect. I made a mistake, and I'm sure you make as many as I do. Please forgive me. I want to come back to you."

Glory narrowed his eyes. "I suppose Patch wasn't enough for you once he was caught. I'm not going to be your slave, Gabrielle."

She shook her head. "Slave? More like you would be my idol, Glory. I love you."

Glory glared at her. "You said the same thing before. Only you broke your vow to me and loved someone else. You broke my heart, and I'm not in a hurry to have you do it again."

She stomped her foot in aggravation. "I promise you that I won't do that again. Please, I will do anything to make you mine again." Glory shook his head. "No, Gabrielle. I won't leave Secret again. I love her, not you. She showed me what true love is."

Gabrielle closed her eyes. "Glory, deep in your heart, I think you still love me. Stay true to your real feeling of love. Secret is nothing. I am everything." Glory snorted angrily.

"NO! I do not love you at all! In your opinion, Secret is the traitor, and you are the princess. In my mind, it's quite opposite! Now leave me, and never return! Stay with your *beloved* Patch!"

With that, Glory marched out of the thicket, and back to the cave. He burst into his room and slammed the oak slab used as a door. Secret jumped up from the bed where she had been sleeping.

"Glory! What on earth?" she exclaimed in surprise. Glory exhaled slowly, and told her about his fight with Gabrielle.

Secret started to cry. "I thought for sure you would leave me, Glory. I didn't know how much you love me."

Glory nodded. "I would rather die than live life without you, Secret. You are my completion. Without you, I am lost." Secret's ears drooped slightly, and she shuddered.

"I had no idea you even sort of loved me. As soon as you went after Gabrielle, I thought I was completely out of the picture. Please, promise me that you will never leave me again!" Glory nodded, "I swear with my whole heart that I will not."

****

The next day, Glory awkwardly muttered to himself as he paced back and forth in front of the cave entrance. .

"I love you, and I really want to… I mean to say…Well, I was thinking that you…I could maybe ask…Oh, man. What am I going to say to her?"

Suddenly, Secret came walking out of the cave to meet him, and Glory motioned her to follow him. He led her to the special thicket, and stood facing her. "Secret, I love you with my whole heart, and I want to ask you to be with me forever. Would you consider me as your mate?"

Secret gasped. "Oh, Glory. What is there to consider?" Glory looked up. "Secret, if you refuse, I will understand. I'm sure that there are much more deserving stallions than me, that will love you as much as I do."

Secret violently shook her head. "No. I would be honored to be your mare. When should we tell your parents?"

Glory laughed. "I hope today isn't too soon."

Secret smiled. "No. Today is just fine."

Glory raced back to the cave, gathered everyone outside, and stood up on the big council rock.

"Everyone, I am honored to say that this lovely mare beside me has agreed to become my mate!"

The herd voiced their approval. The stallions pounded their hooves against the ground, and the mares whinnied.

Novana had tears in her eyes. "My son finally found his mare. I am so happy for you, Glory," she told him.

Fury just nodded to his son. "You have made a wise choice, Glory. I am proud of you."

"Welcome to our family, Secret," Sariavo said with a kind smile.

Glory glanced at Secret, and said, "Let's go to the Indian settlement for our first journey."

Secret drew back in fear. "But, Glory! They will capture us and…" Glory was shaking his head. "Running Fox freed me. I am not his anymore. We are friends."

After much convincing on Glory's part, Secret agreed. The two set off, and stopped at the site of Glory's first herd. The valley was empty, and it made Glory sad.

"This was where I met the herd. They were captured with me." Secret sighed. "I don't understand why you love Running Fox so much, after what he did to you."

Glory sighed. "He taught me about loyalty. Without him, I never would have returned to you." Secret's eyes widened. "Really?" Glory nodded. "He is my best friend."

~ 7 ~

Return to Running Fox

As the pair traveled, they were unaware of a dangerous being trailing them. A huge silvertip grizzly had spotted their trail, and he was determined to catch them. He was about a mile behind them, and closing the gap quickly.

That night, as Glory and Secret dropped off to sleep, he saw them. He was standing on top of the ridge overlooking the valley where they were.

At about midnight, Glory got the feeling that he was being watched. He pretended to sleep, keeping his ears, eyes, and nostrils alert.

The bear charged, and Glory caught its scent just as it came roaring down the valley, barely 100 feet from them. He screamed a challenge, and shoved Secret behind him. She was wide awake now, and screaming in fright. Glory stood his ground as the bear came running towards them, bellowing so loud that it shook the ground where Glory stood.

The silvertip reached out with a mighty paw to knock Glory head over heels into a stump. Glory immediately scrambled to his feet, charging the bear as the huge monster headed for Secret, who was running as fast as she could away up the valley wall.

Glory followed the two, but soon was anguished to see Secret turn into the three-walled trap where the Indians had captured him. He tried to turn the bear away from her, but was rewarded by being slapped across the chest with the long claws.

A minute later, Glory heard Secret screaming. He gasped as the strain of rising from the dirt pulled on his open chest.

Nonetheless, he had to save his mare. He bravely galloped into the trap, screaming angrily, and hit the bear hard across the face with his hooves, and then grabbed one of the tiny ears in his teeth and pulled. The bear roared, and slung his head to the left, flinging Glory.

Suddenly, an arrow sped past the albino stallion into the bear's side, and the bear fell to its knees, growling.

Glory lifted his battered head to see who had saved them, and saw a blurry image of a bronze skinned rider on a spotted horse. It was Running Fox.

The Indian shot another arrow into the bear, and then, satisfied that it was dead, he ran to Glory, who was lying next to a rock he'd been slung into, bleeding and bruised.

Running Fox gently touched the chest wound, and drew back when the stallion snorted in pain. "***White Horse***," the man murmured softly.

Glory heard that voice, and his master's call filled him with a loyal love and the desire to do whatever Running Fox asked of him. He struggled up, and nuzzled the Indian's chest. Secret stayed a few feet away, speechless in awe of the special bond that existed between her protector and this two legged being.

Glory weakly whinnied to his mare, and then wobbled towards the entrance of the trap. Running Fox followed, keeping his hand on the white shoulder, softly talking to him.

"You'll be all right, big boy. I heard all the roaring and screaming, and I knew that it was your voice." Secret slowly followed the tortured stallion, nickering encouragement to him.

When they reached the village, Running Fox led Glory to his tepee. He took a strip from his own deerskin cape, and soaked it in the river. He returned to the stallion and gently cleaned the gashes and cuts.

He told several of the curious braves to run and bring back the dead grizzly. They hurried off, dragging ropes behind their horses to pull the bear.

Running Fox took an eagle bone needle, and slowly threaded horsehair thread through Glory's chest, sealing the open wound. Glory grunted, but didn't try to wiggle away from the soft hands ministering to him.

Secret stood next to him, tears running down her cheeks. "Oh, Glory, you look horrible."

Glory chuckled. "Thank you, very…much. You sure know how to make a sick stallion feel good." Secret laughed softly.

Running Fox stood, after he had finished closing the wound, and walked away, putting his horse back on the tie rope.

Secret stood over Glory, whispering, "A heart to match your own. Those were the first words you ever spoke to me…remember?" Glory drifted off to sleep to the sound of her singing.

******

When Glory awoke, he wondered where he was. Then he saw tepees surrounding him. Secret lay a few feet off, softly speaking to herself in her sleep. He tried to get up, and winced at the pain in his chest. He saw Running Fox coming towards him, and whinnied a weak but meaningful welcome.

The chief laughed. "Hello, Big Boy. Are you feeling better?" Glory shook himself, and buried his nose in Running Fox's arms. The Indian murmured to him and stroked the soft white muzzle. He nodded toward Secret.

"I see you found a mare for yourself, Boy. She was a good choice. Very pretty girl, she is. I've named her Prairie Bird. Do you like it?"

Glory huffed softly in approval.

"I'll take that as a yes!" Running Fox said with a smile.

For a whole week, Running Fox refused to let his patient go anywhere except the creek for water. He told Glory that if he rushed the healing, it could get worse. So, Glory spent his time watching what the Indians did. He watched the squaws stretch hides, cut meat, and build tepees.

He saw the men hunt, and train wild horses. He watched the children play, and run about with puppies.

Glory felt restless because he couldn't be of more help. He tried to give rides to the small children, but Running Fox forbid the children to touch the albino stallion.

Secret spent her time with Glory, or sometimes she went out on hunts with the men, and helped to pull the meat back on a travois.

Glory wished he could accompany the hunting parties, and pull back meat. But his master stood firm, not even letting him go faster than a slow walk.

****

When the wound was completely healed, Running Fox rewarded Glory's patience by galloping him up and down the valley, and having Secret running alongside.

The three loved the feel of the wind whipping against their faces, and the priceless sensation of flying. Secret loved this as much as Glory, and every day, when it was time to gallop, she followed Running Fox around wherever he went, nuzzling him and whinnying until he finally gave in with a laugh at her persistence.

****

After a month had passed, Glory and Secret decided to go home. They spent their last day with Running Fox, galloping and romping around in the dirt piles.

When they left, Running Fox gently touched Glory's feather. "White Horse, my friend," he said softly. He took another eagle feather and tied it in Secret's mane, and then led Glory aside. "White Horse, do not go fast on your way home. Prairie Bird carries a foal that will be born in the spring, and you do not want her to hurt herself."

Glory looked at Secret, and noticed her slightly rounded sides. He pranced in place, so excited about being a father that he almost stepped on Running Fox's bare feet. He nuzzled his friend for the last time, and cantered off to join Secret.

As they journeyed back to the old cave, Glory told Secret what Running Fox had told him. "He said that you are carrying a foal, and that we must not go fast, or you will hurt yourself, or the foal."

Secret sighed. "I wish he hadn't told you. I didn't want you to worry about me."

Glory laughed. "I would have figured it out in a month or two," he teased.

She smiled. "Yes, I'm sure you would have."

****

When they got back to their home, Sariavo and Fury came out to meet them. "Hello! Did you have a good time?" Sariavo asked.

"Oh, yes! Glory got hurt by a bear though," Secret told him.

Fury inspected his son's scar. "Oh, Glory. You always have to tangle with something a lot stronger than you."

Glory snorted. "That silvertip almost got Secret." Sariavo admonished his son, "Fury, you saved Novana from the wolves. You should know what Glory felt."

Fury nodded. "I was just teasing. Glory, your grandmother, Sari, died while you were gone. I'm sorry." Glory looked quickly at his grandfather, who barely was keeping the tears back.

"I'm sorry, Grandpa." Glory took one of the eagle feathers from his mane, and gave it to Sariavo. "Thank you, Glory. Thank you." With that, his grandfather walked back inside the cave.

~ 8 ~

A Foal Arrives

It took Sariavo a few weeks to stop grieving for his beloved mare. The herd left him alone, and the old stallion was grateful. Glory brought him wild grapes every day, and Sariavo was touched that someone was so sorry for him.

He called Glory in to his room a few days after his grandson's return. "Glory, I want to talk to you." Glory stepped in, and lay down on the rock floor. "Glory, I know that I probably seem silly to grieve all this time, but…it is so hard not to."

Glory shook his head. "It doesn't seem silly, Grandpa. I know how special Grandma was to you. I would feel the same way if I lost Secret." The old stallion grinned.

"I noticed Secret has been eating very well," he teased.

Glory laughed. "Yes, she is pregnant. I hope she'll be okay."

Sariavo smiled. "Mares are a lot tougher than we think. A lot of times Sari and Penny have amazed me."

Glory nodded, “But I can still worry. Some mares die having foals.”

Sariavo looked up. “Is that what you are worried about, Glory? She will be fine, you’ll see.” After that, Glory didn’t worry so much, but he still didn’t fully believe that nothing would happen.

****

Soon, Secret’s usually slim sides began filling out, so that she sometimes knocked things over with her belly.

Glory was lying beside her in their room one night, thinking about what Sariavo had told him. “Secret, what will I do if something happens to you,” he asked the buckskin mare.

She rolled over, with no small difficulty, and looked at him. “I am not going to die having a foal, Glory. Mares just like me do it all the time, and they are still healthy. Trust me.”

Glory frowned. “But…” Secret sighed. “Glory, please. I have to have your foal, no matter how much you worry. So go to sleep.”

****

Secret and Glory were walking in the woods, to give Secret some exercise. Suddenly, she stopped, frowned, and then started walking again. A few minutes later, she repeated the movements. Glory looked at her questioningly.

"What's wrong?" Secret shook her head. "I don't know." Glory turned around, "Maybe you should go back to the cave." She nodded, and started back.

Glory followed her, and as soon as they reached the waterfall, Penny and Novana came out. Penny took one look at Secret's face, and hurried her into a large room at the back of the cave.

Novana reassured her panicking son. "Glory, she will be fine. Penny and I will look after her." Then, she turned and trotted after Penny and Secret.

Glory tried swimming, walking, talking, and running to ease his nerves, but nothing prevented his worrying about Secret.

Fury tried to sooth the young stallion, and so did Sariavo, but all Glory could think about was his young mate.

Finally, he heard a soft, shrill whinny come from the large room. He raced to the door, and knocked.

"Come in, Glory," he heard Secret say. He lunged through the doorway, and saw Secret lying on the moss, and curled up next to her, was a tiny dapple-gray filly. Glory sighed with relief.

"You're all right, Secret?"

The young mother laughed. “If exhaustion were a disease, I would be dying.” Glory nodded. “Good, at least you aren’t…or…”

Secret sighed. “Glory, I am fine.” The albino nodded slowly.

******

After two days, the filly was up and about. Glory was stuck trying to think of a name for his daughter. He finally came up with Star Dancer, and he would call her Dancer for short.

Over the next three weeks, Dancer continued to grow and learned new words every day. Her vocabulary now consisted of, yes, no, daddy, mommy, and pickle. Glory had no idea where she had learned pickle, but she sure knew it. She would walk around the cave, stopping everyone and asking, “Pickle, Pickle?”

Dancer loved Sariavo, and always wanted him to tell her stories of his adventures; because he did all the different voices to match the horses and people he had met.

****

Glory watched his daughter grow with love and pride, but something inside of him wanted to travel again. Secret was also restless, pacing the isles between the rooms in the cave. Glory asked his father if he thought Dancer was old enough to go on a journey, and Fury said he didn't know why not. So, Glory packed up his family and headed for the mountains.

They traveled at a slow trot, so Dancer could keep up. She had of course learned more words now, and kept up a steady conversation.

"Mommy, do you know where we are going?" Secret sighed, tired of the constant talking. "No, sweetie, ask Daddy."

So, Dancer marched up to Glory and asked, "Daddy, where are we going?" Glory smiled at her. "Well, we are just kind of walking around. We aren't going anywhere in particular, but at the end of the week we will probably end up at Running Fox's village."

****

Glory and Secret seemed to love traveling, but little Dancer soon grew bored, and drove her parents crazy.

"Are we there yet? Can I have a drink? I'm hungry. We should stop soon. Can we stop now?"

Glory finally said, "Dancer, can we please be quiet for a while? I know you're anxious to get there."

Dancer was silent the rest of the day.

****

At the end of the week, Glory reached a familiar place. He raced up the trail to the top of the ridge overlooking the village, and started to whinny a greeting, but then was stopped.

The teepees were ripped apart and burning. Dead Indians lay all over the ground. Horses writhed on the grass, dying or wounded.

Glory turned to Secret. "Don't let Dancer see this. Dancer, do not look!" Dancer stayed so she couldn't see over the ledge, and Secret came to stand beside Glory.

"Oh! What happened to them?" Glory saw warriors dead on the plain ahead of the village, and noticed the war paint.

"Comanche warriors must have gathered a huge war party and destroyed the village." Secret started to cry.

Glory whirled and galloped full speed towards the tepee of his friend. As soon as he looked inside, Glory saw Running Fox and his wife lying on the floor, blood covering them. Many Deer, Running Fox's wife, was dead, but Running Fox was still breathing slightly.

Glory gently grabbed his master's shirt in his teeth, and slowly pulled the man out of the tepee.
"Whi…"Running Fox murmured weakly. Glory felt tears come to his eyes. He pressed his head into his friend's chest, and felt a weak, yet soft touch on his muzzle. He nickered quietly.

"Whi…te… Horse," Running Fox whispered. Then, the hand slowly fell away from Glory's nose. The stallion suddenly felt a small emptiness in his heart. He knew, then, that his master was gone.

~ 9 ~

An Empty Heart

For the rest of the day, Glory feverishly dug a hole underneath an oak tree, tearing up the soft dirt with his hooves, making a suitable burial place for his master and friend. When he had a big enough hole, he went back to the dead chief and slowly dragged him towards his resting place.

Glory gently pulled him into the hole, and looked at his peaceful face. Running Fox seemed to dream, as if in his sleep. Glory made sure that the Indian wasn't breathing, and then started to push the dirt back in gently with his nose.

When the job was done, Glory wanted to put something over the grave, to symbolize his master's friendship. Then, Glory knew exactly what that symbol should be. He reached around and pulled the feather out of his mane, and stuck it in the mound of dirt.

The long feather moved slightly in the breeze, and Glory felt a whoosh of air enfolding around him.

When he rejoined his family, Glory looked back at the burning village, and felt his heart go half empty. He didn't feel happy anymore, just abandoned, and lonely.

Secret didn't ask any questions when she saw him coming slowly up the trail, covered in dirt, and smoke. She simply nuzzled his nose, and followed him back to the path home.

Glory knew that if she said anything, tears would break loose, and his father had taught him the rule since he was a young colt: ***Stallions do not cry***. Dancer came running up to stand beside him.

"Daddy? Why are you sad?" Glory looked down at her, and tried to smile.

"Someone that Daddy loved very much just died, sweetie. That is why I am sad."

Dancer kissed his shoulder, because that was as high as she could reach, and said, "I'm sorry Daddy. Will he get better soon?"

****

They reached the Six Mares Valley, as Glory had named it, and saw six horses grazing peacefully there. Glory recognized them at once.

"Hello to my family!" he called loudly. The mares lifted their heads and whinnied joyfully. Grace came limping up.

"Hello, White Horse." (Glory had never told them his real name, and they heard Running Fox call him White Horse, so they called him the same)

Glory managed a small grin. "Do you know my real name is Glory?"

Grace shook her head. "No. We know you as White Horse, so White Horse you will stay." The name made Glory's heart ache.

****

Glory and Secret decided to stay with the herd for a short time, because Glory wasn't ready to go home just yet.

Dancer soon had the doting attentions of all the mares in the herd. Grace especially fell in love with the young filly, and spoiled her. Dancer enjoyed the attention of 'Auntie Grace', and spent most of her time with the old mare.

Glory stayed by himself most of the time, and every night in his sleep, he dreamed about the days he'd spent with Running Fox. He was miserable, and no one could talk to him, because he wouldn't say anything.

Secret finally decided to talk to him, so she went to where he was lying in the woods, talking to himself.

Secret lay down next to him, and said, "Glory," softly.

He looked up at her, and shook his head. “Glory, please. Don’t leave me. I’m here. Not dead. And Dancer needs her Daddy. Please come back to us.”

Glory lowered his head, and spoke. “Secret, I cannot face life without him. He was my best friend.”

Secret looked into her mate’s eyes. “I know, but maybe…I could be your best friend. I’m still here. I’m still your mare.”

Glory nodded. “I’m sorry, Secret. I miss him so much, it hurts.” Secret stood, and slowly, so did Glory, and they silently walked back to the herd.

Glory told them that he planned to leave for home in the morning. Secret wholeheartedly agreed.

So the next morning, Secret, Dancer and Glory said their goodbyes and left, never to return to the Indian Village or Six Mares Valley again. Grace agreed to look after the herd until they could find another stallion.

~ 10 ~

Another Sorrow

Sariavo was dead. The old stallion had passed away in his sleep a few days before Glory's return. Fury met him outside with the news, and barely kept his voice. Glory led his mares into the cave, and showed them all to their rooms.

Then he went into his grandfather's room. The old stallion was lying on his moss bed, covered with flowers, feathers, and other small pieces of everything. Fury placed an eagle feather next to his grandsire's body. Glory saw that no one was around, so he let loose the tears that had been dammed up for so long.

Soon, his face was wet, and he started shaking uncontrollably. First Running Fox, and now Sariavo. It was too much. Both had been his advisors and friends, and Glory felt like everything dear to him was being ripped away.

Secret felt helpless. Just when she had brought her husband back to her world, he left it again, and this time he stayed in Sariavo's room, refusing to eat, drink, or speak with anyone.

The buckskin mare was now listless, and didn't like to do much except eat.

Dancer discovered that her mother's milk tasted bitter, and was confused, because it had always been good and healthy.

Finally, Novana decided that her daughter in law was very sick. Secret was very warm, and coughed constantly.

Secret was hurried into her room, and cold water was poured over her. At the end of the day, Novana was getting very worried.

Secret's fever had gotten worse, and she was now wheezing with every breath. The black mare went straight to her son.

"Glory, its Secret. I think she…she is very sick, and she might be dying. Don't leave her alone."

Glory's head shot up, and he raced for his mare's side. Once beside her, he started to pray. "Oh God, don't take her away too. Please."

Glory stayed next to Secret for three days, praying, and watching for any small sign of her getting better.

Nothing happened. Glory thought of the one person who could make his wife better. Sariavo had told him of his old master, Phillip, and how he could heal any horse.

Glory asked Fury if he knew where the man lived. Fury remembered what Sariavo had told him and relayed the information to his son. "But, Glory, be careful. Phillip will be almost fifty some years old. Carry him gently."

Glory set off immediately. He nuzzled Secret, and galloped as hard as he could in the direction of Phillip's house. He passed three towns, and headed for the fourth. The town was small, and Glory found the right farm right away. He sprinted up the driveway, and saw an older man grooming a spotted pony. He lunged for the man.

Phillip looked up, and his eyes got wide when he saw the wild albino stallion running for him. He stepped back. Glory remembered his grandsire saying that this man seemed to understand horses.

Phillip looked at him strangely. "Are you the grandson of Sariavo? Somehow you remind me of him."

Glory nodded his head up and down. Phillip laughed for joy.

"What brings you here?" he asked. Glory came over and nudged the man's arm, and gently pulled at Phillip's shirtsleeve with his teeth.

Phillip seemed to understand that Glory needed him to go somewhere.

Phillip led Glory to a fence, and climbed up on it, and threw his leg over the white stallion's back.

"Goodness! You are much taller than your grandsire."

Glory raced the twenty miles back to the cave, and it was all Phillip could do to hang on. While they were traveling, Glory told his new friend that Sariavo had died. Phillip was silent for the rest of the trip, grieving for his mighty stallion.

When they reached the home of Glory, Phillip jumped down and dashed into the cave. Glory staggered wearily, because he had just galloped almost forty miles, and he was so worn out that he couldn't even lift his head. Fury came out to see him, and Glory tried to ask about Secret, but instead, his knees buckled and he collapsed in exhaustion.

When Glory opened his eyes, he saw a blurry figure standing next to him. He tried to focus on the shape, but he couldn't. "Glory? I'm so happy you're okay." Glory nodded, and the world started to spin. He drifted back into sleep.

While Glory rested, Phillip attended to Secret's every need.

Finally, Glory woke up again, and this time he could see clearly. And what he saw made him want to laugh for joy. Standing beside him, was none other than Secret herself. She was half laughing, half crying. "Oh, Glory. When Fury told me you had collapsed, I thought you were a goner." Glory shakily stood. "Nah. You know me too well. I don't quit."

Secret laughed again, and shook her head. "You aren't as tough as you think you are. I know better," she said.

By gathering bits of information from different people, Glory found out that after he had collapsed, his father had dragged him into his room, and Phillip had predicted that he was fine, just sick with exhaustion from galloping so far.

After that, Secret got better so quickly that Novana and Phillip allowed her to stay with Glory. He also learned that Phillip had gone back to his home, catching a ride from the gelding Jake.

~ 11 ~

Home Free

A month passed and Glory was amazed that he hadn't gotten the urge to travel again. But he realized that everything he wanted or cared about was all right here. Without Running Fox, there wasn't anything that he wanted outside of his home. He had his parents, his friends, his family, and other than that, there wasn't anything he needed.

Glory decided to find Dancer and play with her. She had been restless lately, wanting someone to play with. Grace didn't have time because there were a lot of mares having foals this time of year, so she was busy caring for the newborn babies.

Dancer was standing outside, watching the breeze ruffle through the trees, a bored look on her face. Inahu stood beside her, talking softly.

Glory walked up to the two fillies, and said, "Hey, why all the glum faces?" Inahu looked up, and Glory realized that his little sister was becoming a beautiful young mare. He swallowed hard, not wanting her to grow up and leave him.

She whispered, "I am waiting for someone," and ashamedly turned away. "Ok, out with it. Let me guess that you are waiting for a young stallion?" Inahu blushed. "Well, no not exactly…yes."

Glory grinned. "Ah Ha. You better spill the beans. Where are you going with your steed in shining armor?" Inahu gazed at him angrily. "Glory! I have to start courting sometime. Quit treating me like a baby, please!"

Glory immediately regretted his words. "I'm sorry. I just don't want you to leave me." Inahu stared at him, "Oh, Glory. I'm not going to leave you!"

A few minutes later, a handsome chestnut stallion walked into sight. "Hello, Inahu, ready to go?" Glory's sister followed him into the woods, disappearing among the tall trees. Glory saw that his daughter looked dejected.

"Hey, princess, want to race me?" Dancer looked up. "But, you'll win!" Glory shook his head. "I promise I won't go too fast."

Dancer grinned. "Beat ya!" and raced off towards the wide meadows. Glory bolted after her.

After running a few laps of the meadow, the two horses collapsed in a heap of white, dapple-gray, and legs. Glory tickled Dancer's belly with the whiskers on his nose, and the filly started giggling.

"I like it when you play with me, Daddy," she said. Glory smiled at her.

"I like to play with you. Sorry I've been ignoring you lately."

Dancer shook her head. "That's okay. Is Mommy going to have another baby soon?"

Glory thought a minute. "We are very happy to have you. We'll see happens in the future."

Glory played with Dancer the rest of the day, and promised her that he would sleep under the stars in the meadow with her that night. Dancer squealed and ran to tell Secret that Daddy was going to sleep outside with her.

Secret gave Glory a happy look that said, "I'm glad you are spending time with her. It makes her feel special." Glory grinned back.

After supper, Dancer gave Glory no peace about going outside, but to pass the time, he asked her to go swimming with him. When he got into the water, he felt himself being pulled underwater. He bobbed back to the surface, looking around for the culprit, and saw Dancer, laughing so hard she almost cried. "I dunked you, Daddy!" Glory started to laugh too.

The two of them went out to the meadow and bedded down in the tall grasses.

Dancer asked, "Daddy, can you touch the stars?"

Glory looked at her. "Why do you ask that?"

Dancer smiled innocently. "I was wondering if you could get one for me."

And, as Glory gazed up at the sky toward heaven, he wondered what Running Fox was doing. Maybe, just maybe, he was riding a big bay stallion named Sariavo.

Epilogue

Glory and Secret's new life was full of love and pride as they watched the growth of their foal. The intelligence of Dancer, their filly, was marveled over by the whole herd, and most of all Fury. The older stallion was so proud of his small granddaughter. He was certain that though she was not a stallion, she would play a huge part in the future of the line of the Mighty Stallions.

Meet The Mighty Stallion Mascot:

Looky the Mighty Gelding

Hello, I am an American Quarter Horse/ Pony of Americas gelding. My name is Looky. I am a red roan. My picture is on the back of Mighty Stallion 2 Fury's Journey and on Mighty Stallion 5 A Stallion's Heart!

I was moved around a lot until age 3 and that's when Victoria and her family bought me. Victoria and I are great friends, and we do a lot together. She enjoys riding me bareback, and I love to give rides to two people at once!!!

I love being the Mighty Stallion mascot, even though I'm a gelding. I'm a stallion at heart and that's what counts.

About The Author…

Victoria Kasten was born in 1991. She has loved horses since she could walk. She began taking English riding lessons at age nine, and continued with the lessons until age thirteen.

She has two horses, a mischievous Quarter Horse/Pony of America gelding named Looky, and a beautiful bay registered Quarter Horse mare named Katie.

She discovered her love of writing at age eight, when she wrote a short story called The Wild Mustang. She also began to write poems, two of which were published in a national Christian newspaper. Her first Mighty Stallion book was finished at age twelve and published at age 14.

Victoria hopes to be a full time author after she finishes college. She enjoys many hobbies such as researching Medieval History; singing; and spending time outside on her family's farm with her cats, rabbits, horses and alpacas.

Interested in knowing more about Victoria or her books?

- Check out Victoria's web site: **www.EpicScrolls.com**
    - Find out the latest news on Victoria and her books…
    - See a list of stores that currently carry her books
    - Check out Victoria's appearance and book signing schedule to meet her in person.
    - Email Victoria

Or…

- Write to her at:

5465 Glencoe Ave, Webster, MN 55088

Other Books by Victoria:

❖ Mighty Stallion

Join Fury's father, Sariavo, the mighty stallion, as he embarks on the grand adventure that started it all.

❖ Mighty Stallion 2 Fury's Journey

Sariavo's son, Fury, is determined to carry on his stepfather's line as a Mighty Stallion. Accompanied by his beautiful mate, Novana, Fury strikes out on his own to prove his adulthood and discovers his destiny.

❖ Mighty Stallion 4 Dancer's Dream

Follow the story of Dancer, the daughter of Glory, as she discovers her path as the first mare in the line of Sariavo to carry the bloodline onward.

❖ Mighty Stallion 5 A Stallion's Heart

Two brothers, Shalimar and Storm, set out for their adventures. Time will reunite them as each of them encounter the Pony Express and face a terrible forest fire where one of them must learn the meaning of sacrifice.

❖ IronHeart

Victoria begins her fantasy debut with this non-magical novel for teens and adults. IronHeart is a heart-warming tale of adventure, courage and the strength to persevere, and showcases the meaning of true friendship. (300+ pages.)

Sneak Peek…
Coming Soon…

Mighty Stallion 6 The Civil War (Bonus Edition!)

The sixth book in the series follows the incredible journey of Storm and Kaya's daughter, Miracle. She finds herself captured and in the middle of one of America's greatest conflicts, the Civil War. She becomes the mount of an officer, and she meets a very interesting man… Private Edward Bassett.

Note to Readers: Private Edward Bassett is a direct ancestor of Victoria Kasten. The book will include real stories about him taken from copies of his letters. Mighty Stallion 6 will be a large bonus edition with lots of extra information.

Mighty Stallion Order Form **www.EpicScrolls.com**

PLEASE PRINT:

NAME: ____

ADDRESS: ______________________________________

CITY: __________________ **STATE:** ___________

ZIP: ___________ **PHONE:** __________________

_____ Copies Mighty Stallion 1 @ $8.95 each $________

_____ Copies Mighty Stallion 2 Fury's Journey @ $8.95 each $________

_____ Copies Mighty Stallion 3 Glory's Legend @ $8.95 each $________

_____ Copies Mighty Stallion 4 Dancer's Dream @ $8.95 each $________

_____ Copies Mighty Stallion 5 A Stallion's Heart @ $8.95 each $________

_____ Copies IronHeart @ $14.95 each $________

Postage & handling @ $2.50per book/$1 for Each additional book $________

Minnesota Residents Please add 6.5% Sales Tax $________

Total Amount Enclosed: **$________**

Make Checks payable to: Victoria Kasten

Send to: Epic Scrolls, 5465 Glencoe Ave, Webster, MN 55088